My Big Thank You Note Project

By Jason Valenstein and Margaret Valenstein

Little Stoics Children's Books - Volume 4

For my Mommy who always helps me through BIG PROJECTS.

-MV

For our amazing readers, Alice, Brianne, Carine, Deborah, Leah, Liz, Neha, Marlane, Samantha, Melanie & Edgar, MJ, Tim, and Van. Enjoy with your little ones in the family and at school!

-JV & MV

Reading Note:

It's the little things that matter. Good habits and small tasks add up. Big things happen over time.

Whether it be colorful food and outdoor play for our children's bodies, problem solving and reading for their minds, or small and frequent expressions of gratitude and love in their relationships, all great outcomes they enjoy over time are the culmination of the little choices our children make and the little actions that they take in daily living.

It's the author's hope that this real-life vignette from his family helps someone you love adopt good little habits that let her (or him) achieve something big!

I love my birthday!

Look at all of these presents that I got...

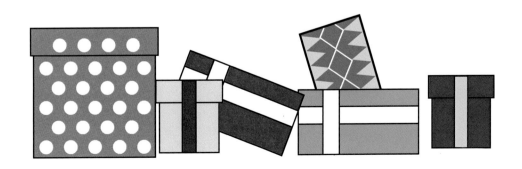

A princess dress.

It is purple with silver flowers and jewels.

A super hero
costume.

A science kit.

(I love mixing things.)

And my soft,
squishy bear...

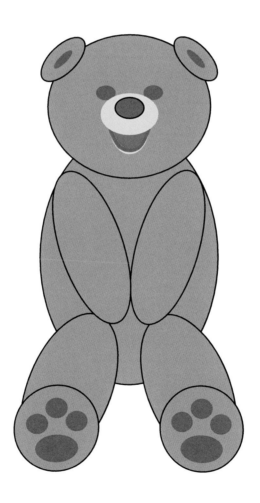

...I will call him Cupcake.

I can snuggle him all day long.

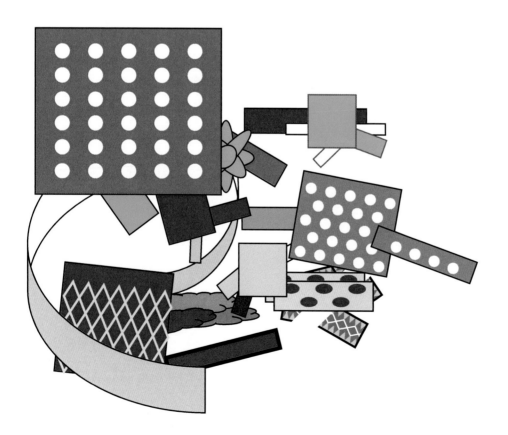

I love all my new
books too!

You are lucky, my dear, for having so many people who gave you so many great presents.

Story Book

Science Book

Magic Book

Picture Book

Story Book

Science Book

Magic Book

Picture Book

How many is that?

Well… from our family there are your Grandparents in Florida, your Grandpa in New York, your Grandma in Texas, your Aunt and Uncle in Texas, your Aunt in Illinois, and you have nine friends in town that each gave you a present….

So, let's see… That's fourteen notes in all.

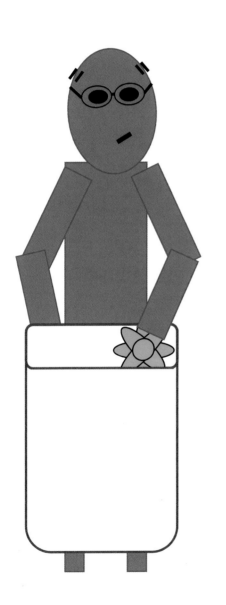

Fourteen?

Fourteen???

Fourteen!!!

That is a BIG PROJECT!
How will I do that?

I'm not a good writer yet
and fourteen is too many...

Do it a little bit at a time, my dear. Saying thank you with your heart is what matters, not straight lines of writing or perfect spelling.

Just focus on that.

I know what to do!

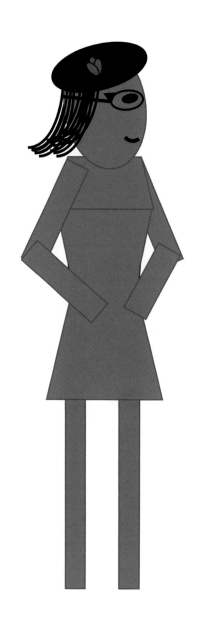

I will focus on what is important, and do my big project a little bit at a time.

I will do one note every morning after breakfast.

I will also do one every evening after dinner.

(Maybe two if I'm feeling up to it.)

My BIG PROJECT will be a bunch of little projects, and I won't get bogged down in the things that I'm not good at yet.

I will learn on the job.
I will also need some help.

That sounds like a great plan. I will help you by making a list of each person and what present they gave you and place it on your red table.

The following morning...

In a minute
Mommy... I need to
finish this note.

The following evening...

One week later...

Mommy, I finished all fourteen of my thank you notes!

Good for you!

I will help you by
addressing them.

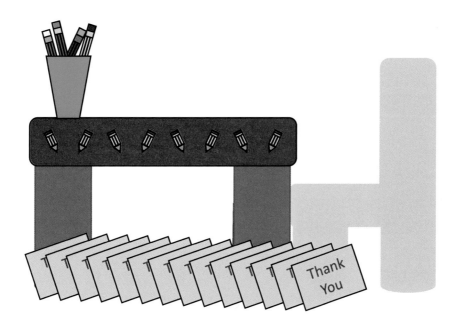

And <u>I</u> will put the stamps on them!

You did it, my dear!

All fourteen thank you notes are ready to go.

You focused on the important thing, saying thank you with your heart, and you worked at your big project little by little until it was complete.

You accepted help along the way too, where you needed it.

We are so proud of how hard you worked and love you so much, our dear sweet darling!

Now I want to put
them into the mailbox!

Available titles in this series include:

Self-Discipline

Equanimity

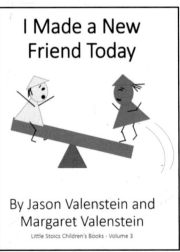

Moral Courage

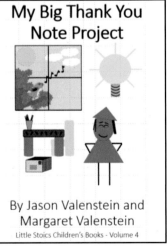

Good Habits